MINOX

Minox is a metallicon evolved from wrecked asteroid-mining vessels, able to pierce solid rock with his powerful drill-arms.

INTELLIGENCE	65
SPEED	58
STRENGTH	80
FREAK FACTOR	75
POWER OF THE UNIVERSE	60

GOR

Gor, a combaton from Planet Attax, has spiked fists that can deliver a serious blow to even the toughest opponent.

INTELLIGENCE	62
SPEED	70
STRENGTH	76
FREAK FACTOR	65
POWER OF THE UNIVERSE	62

BLOK

With an impenetrable body of vulcanite, one of the hardest minerals in the galaxy, Blok is virtually impossible to get past.

INTELLIGENCE	52
SPEED	58
STRENGTH	82
FREAK FACTOR	74
POWER OF THE UNIVERSE	57

CORROSON

Corroson is an acidon ogre dripping with slime from the fuming swamps of IKT-9, whose corrosive grip can burn through metal.

INTELLIGENCE	56
SPEED	62
STRENGTH	74
FREAK FACTOR	85
POWER OF THE UNIVERSE	74

www.alieninvaders.co.uk

www.alieninvaders.co.uk

www.alieninvaders.co.uk

www.alieninvaders.co.uk

ALIEN
INVADERS

Don't miss any of the titles
in the ALIEN INVADERS series:

ROCKHEAD: THE LIVING MOUNTAIN

INFERNOX: THE FIRESTARTER

ZILLAH: THE FANGED PREDATOR

HYDRONIX: DESTROYER OF THE DEEP

ATOMIC: THE RADIOACTIVE BOMB

KRUSH: THE IRON GIANT

JUNKJET: THE FLYING MENACE

MINOX: THE PLANET DRILLER

ZIPZAP: THE REBEL RACER

TANKA: THE BALLISTIC BLASTER

www.kid

04757503

ALIEN INVADERS: MINOX, THE PLANET DRILLER
A RED FOX BOOK 978 1 849 41238 4

First published in Great Britain by Red Fox,
an imprint of Random House Children's Publishers UK
A Random House Group Company

This edition published 2012

1 3 5 7 9 10 8 6 4 2

Text and illustrations copyright © David Sinden,
Guy Macdonald and Matthew Morgan, 2012
Cover and interior illustrations, map and gaming cards by Dynamo Design
Designed by Nikalas Catlow

The right of David Sinden, Guy Macdonald and Matthew Morgan
to be identified as the author of this work has been asserted in accordance
with the Copyright, Designs and Patents Act 1988.

The Random House Group Limited supports the Forest Stewardship
Council (FSC®), the leading international forest certification organization.
Our books carrying the FSC label are printed on FSC®-certified paper.
FSC is the only forest certification scheme endorsed by the leading
environmental organizations, including Greenpeace.
Our paper procurement policy can be found at
www.randomhouse.co.uk/environment.

MIX
Paper from
responsible sources
FSC
www.fsc.org   FSC® C016897

Set in Century Schoolbook

Red Fox Books are published by
Random House Children's Publishers UK,
61–63 Uxbridge Road, London W5 5SA

www.kidsatrandomhouse.co.uk
www.randomhouse.co.uk

Addresses for companies within The Random House Group Limited can be
found at: www.randomhouse.co.uk/offices.htm

THE RANDOM HOUSE GROUP Limited Reg. No. 954009

A CIP catalogue record for this book is available from
the British Library.

Printed and bound by CPI Group (UK) Ltd,
Croydon, CR0 4YY

ALIEN INVADERS

MAX SILVER

MINOX
THE PLANET DRILLER

RED FOX

THE GALAXY

Cosmo's route ----

DELTA QUADRANT

GAMMA QUADRANT

STARFLIGHT SPACESHIP
MANUFACTURING COMPANY

PLANET SYN-NOVA

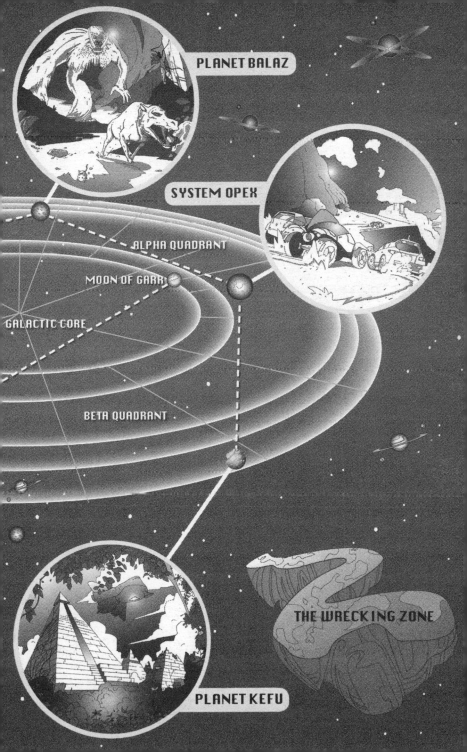

PLANET BALAZ

SYSTEM OPEX

ALPHA QUADRANT

MOON OF GARR

GALACTIC CORE

BETA QUADRANT

THE WRECKING ZONE

PLANET KEFU

RESISTANCE IS FUTILE, EARTHLINGS!

MY NAME IS KAOS, AND MY WAR WITH YOUR
GALAXY IS ENTERING A NEW PHASE...

THE YEAR IS 2121 AND I HAVE JOINED
FORCES WITH METALLICON ALIENS FROM
THE UNIVERSE'S WRECKING ZONE.
THEY HAVE THE POWER OF LIVING
MACHINES, AND I AM PROGRAMMING THEM
TO INVADE YOUR GALAXY.

YOUR SECURITY FORCE, G-WATCH,
WILL BE POWERLESS TO DEFEND YOU, AND
ITS EARTHLING AGENT, COSMO SANTOS,
WILL BE ANNIHILATED ALONG WITH HIS
FRIENDS.

RESISTANCE IS FUTILE, EARTHLINGS.
THE GALAXY WILL BE MINE!

INVADER ALERT!

On Planet Balaz, Professor Vorp crawled down a narrow underground tunnel on his pincers and knees, shining his head torch into a large cavern up ahead.

"We're almost there, R6," he said, glancing back at the lights of an explorobot walking behind on suckered legs. "Keep up."

"Coming, Professor," R6 replied in its computerized voice.

Professor Vorp reached the cavern and stood up, stretching his long Diluvian arms. He looked up at the ceiling and walls, his head torch illuminating red mosses, furry lichen, insects, molluscs and even scurrying reptiles. "R6, log our co-ordinates and let's begin recording these plants and creatures."

The robot whirred. "Investigation point nine. Depth twenty-two metres," it relayed. A sampling tube extended from a tank on its back and, with short sucking sounds, it hoovered up a sample of each insect species.

"That's it, R6," Professor Vorp said. "We can observe them in the zoo-lab back on the spaceship." He took a handheld holo-cam out of his pocket and snapped holographs of fork-tailed lizards that were scuttling across the walls. "The Institute will be amazed at our findings."

Professor Vorp and his explorobot, R6,

were on an expedition to Planet Balaz for the Galactic Institute of New Alien Life as part of an ongoing study to document the planet's unique underground life forms.

At the far end of the cavern, the professor noticed a wide tunnel sloping steeply away. Curious, he shone his torch down into another chamber below; it was overgrown with fleshy plants, the likes of which he'd never seen before. Each had large mouth-like pods writhing on long twisted stalks. One pod snapped up a fork-tailed lizard and gobbled it down whole.

"R6, there's a new species of carnivorous plant down here," the professor called, edging down the sloping tunnel to get a better view. He stopped short of the plants and, gripping a rock with one pincer to stop himself falling into them, reached out his holo-cam to take a few holographs. *Click! Click! Click!*

"Be careful, Professor," R6 called from the top of the slope.

"I'm just taking a few shots," Professor Vorp replied. *Click! Click! Click!*

BOOOOM! Suddenly there came a deafening sound from above, and the walls and ceiling shuddered. The professor lost his grip and almost tumbled down the slope, dropping his holo-cam as he steadied himself. He saw it fall amongst the plants below, where it was snapped up and eaten.

"What was that, R6?" the professor called, peering back into the upper cavern.

But his words were drowned out by the sound of a roaring engine. Slabs and boulders started falling from above, knocking R6 to the ground. Professor Vorp watched, horrified, as a monstrous alien with huge spinning drill-arms tore through the cavern's roof, eyes blazing in a caged metal skull.

The professor lurched backwards in shock and, losing his grip, tumbled into the flesh-eating plants below.

As a large plant pod gripped him, he heard the huge alien roar, "I am Minox, and I am programmed to DRILL!"

CHAPTER ONE

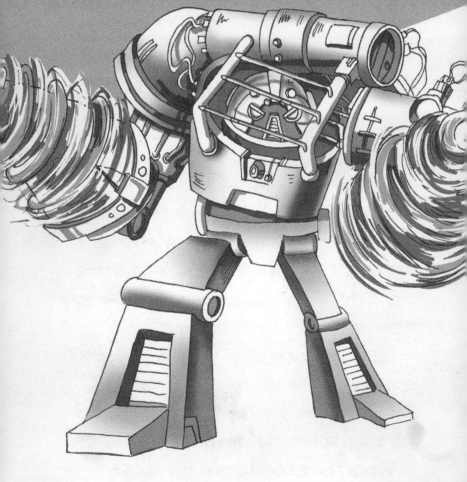

A BARREN PLANET?

"OK, Cosmo, try this," Agent Nuri said. "Ten, nine, eight, seven, *verva*, *vox*—"

"*Verva? Vox?* No, I'm still not hearing you right, Nuri," Cosmo replied. "Can you take over while I sort this out?"

Nuri took control of the Dragster 7000 spaceship from the co-pilot's seat, and Cosmo removed his space helmet, tilted his head to one side and tapped it twice.

From the control desk, the ship's

brainbot, Brain-E, bleeped. "Let me help you, Master Cosmo," it said, climbing onto Cosmo's shoulder and extending a pincer probe towards his ear. "Hold still."

Cosmo felt the cold metal probe extending into his skull. Then it retracted, pulling out a wriggling orange worm.

"Just as I suspected – your wordsworm has got itself in a twist," Brain-E said, pointing to a knot in the worm's middle. "No wonder it's making mistakes."

Wordsworms were standard kit for galactic travellers, placed inside the ear to translate between the millions of languages spoken in the galaxy. Four times in the last hour, Cosmo's worm had mistranslated words, causing confusion between him and his Etrusian co-pilot, Agent Nuri.

Cosmo unknotted the worm, wiped some earwax off it, then popped it back into his ear, feeling it wriggle deep inside again.

"Is it working OK now?" Nuri asked.

Cosmo understood her clearly this time. "It seems to be," he said, replacing his helmet. "Co-ordinates please."

"Planet Balaz is about 150,000 Earth kilometres southwest of here in the Alpha Quadrant," Nuri said.

"Roger that," Cosmo replied, taking back control of the ship and powering it past a diamond-shaped star system. "OK, let's go save the galaxy."

Cosmo, Nuri and Brain-E were on a mission for the galactic security force G-Watch to battle five alien invaders under the command of the outlaw Kaos.

Each was a powerful metallicon android, half living, half machine, from a distant space dump known as the Wrecking Zone. So far Cosmo had defeated two of them: Krush, the iron giant, and Junkjet, the flying menace. Now he was off to Planet Balaz to face the third, identified by G-Watch scanners as Minox.

"What do we know about this invader, Brain-E?" Cosmo asked.

"Minox is evolved from wrecked asteroid-mining vessels, with drill-arms able to pierce solid rock."

"Solid rock!"

"Planet Balaz straight ahead," Nuri said, looking up from the navigation console.

Cosmo tried to remain calm as their destination came into view: an isolated black planet. Flying into its atmosphere, he set the spacescreen to zoom mode; the planet's surface appeared desolate and barren. "Why would Kaos send an invader to this place? There's nothing here," he said.

"I suspect because Balaz is a Great Wonder of the galaxy," Brain-E explained. "Technically it is not a planet at all, but the largest living organism in existence."

"Living organism?" Cosmo said, amazed.

"Yes. In recent times scientists have observed that Balaz is growing. Investigations have revealed it to be a huge spherical creature, host to all kinds of other life forms that live within it."

Cosmo flew the Dragster low, shining the searchlights onto Balaz's cracked surface. "So I'm looking at its skin?"

"That's right, Master Cosmo."

"Get ready to land," Nuri interrupted. "G-Watch scanners indicate Minox beamed in just a few kilometres east of here."

It's crunch time, Cosmo thought, checking Balaz's environment and preparing to land:

PLENTIFUL OXYGEN ■ ■ ■ TEMPERATURE TEN DEGREES CENTIGRADE ■ ■ ■ GRAVITY NORMAL ■ ■ ■

Cosmo felt his courage returning, and his spacesuit, the Quantum Mutation Suit, started to glow. It was energized by a power inside him – the power of the universe – and enabled him to mutate into alien forms to fight his opponents.

Below, a crater came into view where Balaz's skin had been opened up by some large impact. "This must be where Minox struck," Cosmo said. There was no sign of the invader now – just a space research ship nearby, and a small robot clambering out of the rubble.

Brain-E bleeped in alarm. "According to my databank, a Professor Vorp of the Galactic Institute of New Alien Life is currently exploring Balaz. That robot must be his companion explorobot."

"So where's the professor now?" Cosmo asked, scanning the rubble. The Dragster touched down and he opened the cockpit door and ran over to the crater. He and Nuri scrambled down to the explorobot and together pulled it out, setting it back on its suckered feet.

"Monster crashed down and drilled underground," the explorobot said.

"Professor Vorp trapped. Investigation point nine. Depth twenty-two metres."

"He must be under this lot," Nuri said, gesturing to the mass of rubble in the crater. "We'll need to clear a way through."

But the rocks looked heavy, and moving them would be slow work. "Brain-E, could you check this explorobot is OK," Cosmo asked, and as Nuri began removing rubble from the crater, searching for Professor Vorp, Cosmo looked for a quicker way down, fearing for the professor if Minox was down there too. Around the crater, within Balaz's crust, he noticed cracks wide enough for a person to fit through, like vertical shafts into the planet. "Nuri, keep clearing. I'm going to try another way."

Cosmo squeezed down into a shaft at the crater's edge, lowering himself carefully. Down he climbed through darkness, dropping into a tunnel just big enough to crawl along on his elbows and knees. He unclipped the plasma torch from his utility belt and switched it on, sending fork-tailed lizards scuttling. The tunnel led to an underground chamber full of tall writhing plants with mouth-like pods that opened and closed. Cosmo gasped, seeing a space boot lying on the ground among them. "Professor Vorp, are you in here?" he called.

CHAPTER TWO

DANGER UNDERGROUND

Cosmo shone his torch into the darkness, seeing plants writhing in its beam. His arm knocked a bristly stem, and a pod lunged down at him. He dodged as it snapped shut centimetres from his head. Cosmo wriggled commando-style through the tall plants to where the space boot lay. It was torn and chewed. *These plants are carnivorous!* he realized.

He kept still, hearing growling sounds

coming from the plants' pods, and noticed they were drooling purple saliva, a glob of which dripped onto his arm. "Professor Vorp, are you in here?" he called, growing anxious.

There was no answer, so very slowly he started crawling between the plants again, looking for the professor, being careful not to touch their stems and trigger another attack. He came across a mangled holo-cam, wet with saliva. "Professor, where are you?" he called, sweeping his torchbeam around in panic.

He had reached the bottom of a steep slope; the top was blocked by rubble fallen from a chamber above. From close by came a muffled cry. He shone his torch towards the sound and gasped, seeing two legs sticking out of a plant pod; one with a space boot on and one without, a pincered foot quivering. *Professor Vorp's being eaten!* he realized. Cosmo rushed

over and reached up, taking hold of the
professor's legs. He pulled, and a low
growl came from the plant. With a
sucking sound, the professor slid out and
the pod belched. Cosmo steadied himself,
ensuring that neither he nor the
professor stumbled into another plant.

"Eeergh . . . blurgh . . ." Professor Vorp
spluttered, wiping slimy purple saliva off
his face. "Bleeaa-thank you," he said.

"G-Watch agent Cosmo Santos at your service. Your explorobot told us you were down here. Are you OK?"

"I will be when we get out of here," the professor replied, glancing nervously at the hungry plants.

Cosmo looked up the slope, hearing scraping sounds coming from the rubble that was blocking the exit. Just then, a shaft of daylight pierced the darkness. "There you are," a voice said. It was Nuri. She had managed to dig her way down through the rubble. She looked aghast at the slime-covered professor. "You're alive!" she said.

"Thanks to your friend here," the professor replied.

Nuri stepped down the slope. "What happened to you?" she asked.

"Something attacked from above," the professor explained fearfully. "An alien being, but machine-like and terrible. It drilled through Balaz's rock, collapsing the cavern I was exploring, and I fell into these plants. I didn't see much after that."

Cosmo shone his torch at a vast hole drilled into the chamber wall, leading further downwards, leaving the plants mangled and broken around it. "The alien's an invader called Minox, Professor Vorp, and it looks like he's gone deeper," he said. "What's down there?"

"The planet's inner workings," the professor replied. "Caves and tunnels, most of them still unexplored."

"Professor, if you're well enough to rest up at the surface, my friends and I will go after Minox straight away," Cosmo said.

"Don't worry about me," the professor insisted. "It's Balaz that needs your help now, to save it from this invader."

"We'll do our best," Cosmo said.

As Professor Vorp clambered up the slope, Brain-E came scuttling down like a spider. "Your explorobot is OK, Professor," it said as it passed. "And I've downloaded some data from its hard-drive to help us here on Balaz."

"Good luck," Professor Vorp replied.

Cosmo summoned his courage, and his Quantum Mutation Suit glowed. "OK, team. Let's get this invader."

They stepped carefully past the plants and through the large drill-hole in the chamber wall, descending into the darkness in pursuit of Minox.

CHAPTER THREE

INNER WORKINGS

The drill-hole led into a sloping tunnel,
and the G-Watch agents crept down it,
shining their torches at lush alien plants
and fungi growing out of the rock. Some
gave a phosphorescent glow in the
darkness. Many had been trampled by
the invader as he'd passed.

   The tunnel teemed with alien
creatures too: stalk-eyed frogs peeped
from hidey-holes, and colourful winged

insects flitted through the torchlight.

Cosmo had been caving underground on Earth with his dad, who'd been a G-Watch agent too when he was alive, but it had been nothing like this. The air within Balaz was warm, and strange gurgling sounds echoed from the depths. Cord-like fibres reached out of the walls, feeling him as he passed. Curious, he let them play across his gloved hands. "What are these, Brain-E?" he asked.

Brain-E bleeped. "According to the Galactic Institute's records in my databank, those are feeler hairs, Master Cosmo, part of Balaz's nervous system. They're gathering information, checking you out."

"Does Balaz have a brain?" Cosmo asked.

"Many brains, you could say. The feeler hairs send information to nerve centres deeper underground."

The tunnel suddenly constricted, its walls squeezing closer as a hot wind blew

through Cosmo's open visor onto his face.

"What's going on, Brain-E?" Nuri asked.

"It's Balaz breathing, Miss Nuri."

The tunnel widened again, and Cosmo felt the wind blowing on his back this time, as if the planet was inhaling. The wind rustled the feeler hairs and plants.

"These tunnels act as ventilation shafts, drawing oxygen into the planet," the little brainbot continued. It shone a light on the wall, illuminating a network of thin tubes filled with black liquid running through the rock. "Blood vessels in Balaz's rock absorb the oxygen and circulate it throughout the body."

"That black stuff in the rock is blood?" Cosmo asked, amazed.

"Technically it's more like the sap of a plant, but yes, the human equivalent would be blood."

Cosmo continued to follow Minox's trail, noticing more feeler hairs that were twining around trampled plants and pulling them out of the tunnel through cracks in the walls. "Freaky!" he said, shining his torch.

"That's dead matter being taken to be digested," Brain-E explained.

Really freaky, Cosmo thought.

He came to another enormous drill-hole in the tunnel wall where the invader had smashed through. He shone his torch into a slimy cavern with yellow goo hanging in gloopy strands from its ceiling. He stepped in gingerly, pulling down his visor then parting a curtain of slime with his gloves. His boots squelched, and slime dripped onto his helmet.

"Urgh," Nuri said, following him in. "What is this place?"

"This is a mucus gland," Brain-E said, scuttling up to her shoulder.

"Mucus! Like snot, you mean?"

"Similar, yes. There are many mucus glands near the surface of the planet."

Cosmo squelched through the ruptured chamber, his torch illuminating alien toads hopping in the slime, licking it with long flicking tongues.

"This is revolting," Nuri said, pulling a gloopy strand off her spacesuit.

Brain-E bleeped. "Tread carefully, Miss Nuri – I mustn't get mucus in my workings."

"It's leaking from the chamber," Cosmo added, heading for a second drill-hole in the far wall, where mucus was spilling out into a tunnel of purple moss. He shone his torch up and down the tunnel, looking for the invader, and saw flying alien insects flitting in a green mist.

Nuri shone her torch too. The mist was seeping into the tunnel through another large hole in its wall about twenty metres away. "Over there," she said, pointing.

Brain-E's scanner lights flashed. "Be careful. This mist is acidic!"

They stepped cautiously down the tunnel, noticing that the mist was making the moss on the walls wilt. Minox's drill-hole led into a cavernous chamber containing a lake of green liquid, from which the green mist was rising.

"According to the Institute's records, this is a stomach chamber," Brain-E told them.

"Balaz has a stomach?" Cosmo asked, surprised.

"All living organisms have to eat, Master Cosmo."

The stomach looked like a swamp. Their torch beams lit crooked trees growing from the water; some had toppled where the alien invader had smashed his way through.

"Come on – Minox went this way," Cosmo said, stepping inside. His legs sank into the soupy stomach juices and he started to wade across.

Nuri followed with Brain-E on her shoulder. "Master Cosmo, we mustn't spend too long in here or these juices could dissolve us," the brainbot cautioned. "Only a very small number of rare species can survive in such acidic conditions."

Cosmo noticed alien bats flitting through the mist, and the stomach juices rippling as eel-like creatures slithered past his legs.

"It's creepy in here," he said.

Dead plant matter was being drawn through the walls high above, and was falling into the juices, dissolving. Cosmo even saw bones. Then the stomach walls heaved, causing the juices to churn.

"What's going on?" Nuri asked, shining her torch into the murky swamp.

Cosmo noticed a slick of black engine oil on the surface of the stomach juices. "I think Minox must have given Balaz an upset stomach," he said.

"It's not only Balaz he's harming," Nuri added. "The creatures that live here are suffering too." She reached a hand out towards a purple bat that was struggling among the branches of a toppled tree. "Out you come, little fellow," she said, rescuing it from the swamp.

The bat shook its wings to dry itself, then fluttered up into the mist.

Cosmo's torchbeam shone on another drill-hole at the far end of the stomach where juices were draining out. "Minox went that way," he said, wading over and shining his torch into another vast cavern. It was like looking down through the roof of a cathedral filled with crisscrossing cables that pulsed with neon light. "What is this place, Brain-E?"

The brainbot bleeped as it checked its databank. "This is a nerve centre, Master. Those pulsing cables are Balaz's nerves."

Minox had clearly drilled down through

the cables; some hung broken and sparking, with stomach acid dripping onto them causing them to fizz.

Nuri unclipped a handheld scanner from her utility belt and pointed it down into the cavern, taking a reading. "I'm detecting a hazardous high-voltage charge."

"Well, we need to go that way," Cosmo said, unclipping a grappling gun from his utility belt. He shot its hooked end into the chamber ceiling, then gave its cord a tug to check it was secure.

Brain-E bleeped. "Be careful not to touch the nerves, Master Cosmo. You'll get a strong electric shock."

Cosmo started abseiling down; Nuri followed close behind with Brain-E now clamped to her wrist.

There's no getting away, Minox, Cosmo thought determinedly. *Wherever you go, we're right behind you.*

CHAPTER FOUR

DEEPER

Cosmo abseiled between the sparking
nerves, taking care not to touch them. He
could see where Minox had crashed
through: many nerves were torn, their
ends shooting sparks over his spacesuit.
He heard an electric hum, then suddenly
an angry *hisssss* as a giant glowing
spider came stalking along the
crisscrossed cables. "Uh-oh. It looks like
we've got company, Nuri," he called up.

The spider picked its way along the
electric nerves, seemingly unaffected by
their high voltage. It appeared to be a
predator, using the nerves as a web,
hunting for prey.

"It looks like some kind of electrachnid," Nuri whispered, abseiling carefully down towards Cosmo.

"Oh, I don't want to become spider food," Brain-E whimpered, clinging tightly to her wrist.

Steadily Cosmo lowered himself further, trying not to make any sudden movements.

Nuri followed – but so did the creature. It scuttled closer, the nerves crackling as it moved across them.

Suddenly there came a sound of flapping wings as two bats swooped into the cavern. One flew straight down past Cosmo while the other struck a nerve; sparks flared, and immediately the spider lunged out, snatching the bat in its jaws.

"Quick – let's get out of here," Cosmo said. He sped up, but as he did, a broken nerve whipped across his arm, showering him with electric sparks and giving him a shock. He lost his grip and dropped like a stone, crashing against nerve fibres, his Quantum Mutation Suit sparking and flashing, more shocks zapping him as he tumbled to the floor.

Nuri and Brain-E quickly clambered down after him.

"Cosmo, are you OK?" Nuri asked.

Cosmo got to his feet and looked up. Dazed, he watched the spider chomping on its catch. "I'm doing better than that bat," he said.

He looked down again, feeling something scuttle across his space boot. He shone his plasma torch on the ground and saw an eyeless orange rat scurrying across the chamber floor towards another large drill-hole. "Minox has gone deeper, Nuri," he said, pointing.

The drill-hole tunnelled down through a soft, cheese-like substance.

"What is this stuff?" Nuri asked, kneeling down to feel it.

Brain-E slid a probe down into the wall of the drill-hole. "It's fat. One of Balaz's food stores – a vital source of energy."

Cosmo began clambering down the fatty wall, following Minox's trail deeper. The fat felt slippery and soft; it was like climbing down white jelly. It wobbled as he pushed his arms and boots in, trying to get a hold. Grease smeared his visor, making it difficult to see.

"Watch out, Cosmo – more rats incoming!" Nuri called from above him.

Cosmo felt them run over his helmet and down his Quantum Mutation Suit. "It looks like they've sniffed out the fat."

The rats were swarming in from the opening that Minox had drilled, greedily helping themselves to Balaz's fat stores.

"Hey, shoo!" Cosmo yelled, trying to brush them away, but it was no use; the fat store was open now and the rats were hungry.

"We've got to stop Minox before he
drills holes in everything," Nuri cried.
"Balaz is suffering!"

Being careful not to slip, they hurried
down as quickly as they could, dropping
into a large tunnel where they sank
knee-deep in brown sludge. A putrid

stench filled the air. Even with his visor closed, it made Cosmo's eyes water.

Nuri wrinkled her nose. "I don't know where we are but it sure stinks," she said.

Brain-E's lights flashed. "We appear to be in a biological waste dump. Minox's route has opened Balaz's bowels," it said.

"Oh great, that's all we need," Cosmo replied, trying not to slip as he waded off to look for the invader.

"Wait a second, Cosmo – I can hear something," Nuri called, her Etrusian ears twitching.

Cosmo stopped to listen too, but his Earthling ears were less sensitive than hers. IIe felt tiny vibrations through the soles of his boots and noticed ripples on the surface of the sludge. A vibrating hum was coming from deep below.

"That's the sound of drills!" Nuri cried. "It's Minox, Cosmo."

"He must be burrowing deeper right

now!" Cosmo said. "Search for where he went down."

They hurried through the brown muck, shining their torches into side tunnels, looking for the route that Minox had taken. But there was no sign of a drill-hole anywhere.

"Any hole he drilled would probably have been clogged up by this waste," Nuri said.

Brain-E bleeped from her wrist. "I'm afraid it does look like we've lost his trail."

Cosmo listened. The sound of Minox's drilling was getting fainter as the invader went deeper still. "Where do you think he's heading?" Cosmo muttered.

"I don't know, but we have to find a way down too," Nuri replied, peering into the mouth of a cavern. She shone her torch inside – and froze. In the cavern stood a huge hairy beast, shovelling sludge greedily into its mouth, feeding on the waste. The creature turned, startled by Nuri's torchlight, and grunted threateningly. It had dirty yellow tusks, angry eyes and a green warty face.

Cosmo stepped to Nuri's side and whispered to Brain-E on her wrist. "What *is* that thing?"

"Oh dear," Brain-E replied, checking its databank. "According to the Institute's records, it's a species of cave troll."

"Back away slowly," Nuri instructed.

The troll roared at them, its tusks protruding like spears from its lower jaw.

"I'll use the Quantum Mutation Suit to transform and protect us if it charges," Cosmo said.

"No, Cosmo," Nuri replied. "You must save your energy for the battle with Min—" But before she could finish, the troll bounded towards them on its knuckles, splashing through the brown sludge. "Run!" she yelled.

They fled through the waste as fast as they could, the troll lumbering after them on all fours, splashing and grunting.

"This way," Cosmo said, pulling Nuri through a curtain of roots into a side tunnel, hoping to lose the troll. They raced round a bend, but it only led them to further danger – a vast drop. They skidded to an abrupt halt, almost running over the edge of a cliff. Cosmo looked down and then back. "Uh-oh – now we're trapped!"

He shone his torch over the cliff edge but the drop was so huge that his torch beam didn't reach the bottom. He could see vines dangling over the edge, with golden fruit like large plums growing on them. It appeared to be a vertical ventilation shaft to the planet's core. Cosmo heard snorting from the troll, which was still searching for them in the tunnel behind. "Climb down these vines, Nuri," he whispered. "Quick!"

They scrambled over the edge of the
cliff, holding tightly to the vines, and
dimmed their torches in the hope that
the troll wouldn't find them. From below
came a faint sound like a drum being
struck: *baboom . . . baboom . . . baboom . . .*

"What's that noise, Nuri?" Cosmo
whispered.

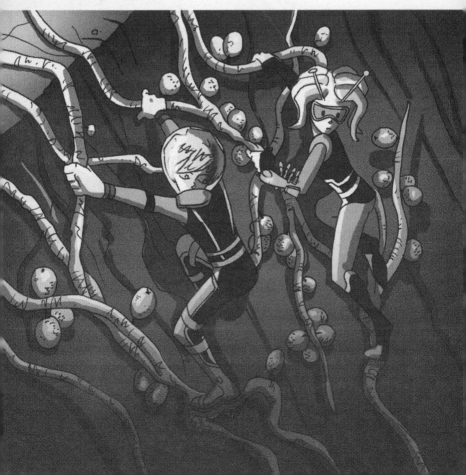

"It sounds like the planet's heartbeat," she replied.

"Planet Balaz has a heart?"

Brain-E bleeped. "No data exists in the Institute's records, but given that Balaz is a living organism, there is every likelihood that it does."

Cosmo had an alarming thought. "And what would happen if someone was to drill through that heart, Brain-E?"

"Then the heart would stop beating and Balaz would die."

"Nuri, that must be where Minox is heading. He's going down towards Balaz's heart!"

Suddenly loud stomping footsteps sounded above their heads, and the vines that they were clinging to shook violently.

"*Ug! Umph!*" It was the cave troll, reaching down from the clifftop to grab hold of them!

CHAPTER
FIVE

THE VICTORY BANQUET

Far beyond the galaxy, in the cockpit of
the battleship *Oblivion*, the five-headed
outlaw Kaos peered at a bank of digital
monitors. He was checking data being
relayed from a circuit board that he'd
implanted in the invader Minox.

"How are Minox's vital signs?" Kaos's
third head asked eagerly.

"Pulse strong," his first head replied.

"Drill revs high," his second head added.

"Excellent," the third head said.

"Oil levels sufficient," said the fourth.

"Brain waves strong," muttered the fifth.

"Look at him go!" the third head spat.

Kaos's five heads leaned towards a monitor showing live images being relayed from a camera behind Minox's eyes; his massive spinning drills were ripping through rock.

"He'll soon reach his target," Kaos's third head said. "And when he kills Balaz, the galaxy's largest living organism, everyone will fear our strength, and G-Watch will

submit to our demands." The third head glanced smugly at the others. "Cause for celebration, I think. Wugrat, come here!"

The cockpit door opened a little and a purple rat scurried in.

"Wugrat, prepare a victory banquet," Kaos's third head ordered.

Wugrat squeaked nervously. "Eeeek."

"What do you mean, 'It's too soon'? My plan is foolproof!"

"Eeek eeek eeeeek eek!"

"Yes, Wugrat, I know that G-Watch will be in pursuit! But I have programmed Minox to deal with them. Now get cooking!"

The third head turned to the others. "By the time our driller killer has finished with the Earthling boy, he'll be so full of holes that even his mother won't recognize him! Victory is in our grasp! It's so close I can taste it."

* * *

Back on Planet Balaz, the three friends clung to the vines on the cliff face, the troll's hairy arm reaching down, groping for them.

"Shoo, troll!" Nuri cried, bashing its finger with her fist.

"Oh, Master Cosmo, what are we going to do?" Brain-E asked.

The troll shook the vine angrily, and golden fruit rattled down from it. Cosmo heard splashes far below as the fruit landed. *We must be above water*, he realized. He thought quickly. *With the cave troll above us, there's no way up, and we need to follow Minox down.* "On the count of three, jump!" he said.

"Are you serious, Cosmo?" Nuri cried.

"Trust me. One . . . two . . . three!"

Cosmo, Nuri and Brain-E let go of the vines and dropped into the darkness below, falling down and down and down. "Whoaaaaaaaaaaaaaaaaaaaa!"

They plunged deep into a river and
swirled underwater, then surfaced among
bobbing golden fruit being washed along
in the current. Cosmo heard the cave troll
roaring with frustration from the top of
the cliff as the current washcd thcm
away downriver, further into the planet.

Cosmo's Quantum Mutation Suit kept
him dry as he swept along. He shone his
torch onto the water's surface – it was
black. "This isn't water – it's Balaz's
blood!" he said.

"We appear to have landed in a river-like blood vessel, Master Cosmo," Brain-E spluttered, clinging tightly to Nuri's shoulder. "A major vein, by the looks of it."

Cosmo shone his torch. The vein was wide, with rocky walls, and flowed towards a huge yellow organ up ahead. "What's

that, Brain-E?" Cosmo asked, pointing to it.

"I believe that's Balaz's liver," the brainbot replied.

The river swept them into a tunnel, the current bumping them against the liver's yellow flesh as they wound through it then came out again on the other side.

Cosmo saw golden vine fruit swirling in the blood ahead. "Whirlpool!" he cried.

He kicked hard, trying to swim against the pull of the current, but it was too strong. The whirlpool took hold of him and Nuri, and spun them round and round. Cosmo felt himself being dragged under by its pull, as if he was being flushed down a plug hole. He was sucked feet first into a narrow rocky tube. Down he shot, spiralling round and down like a corkscrew, black liquid swirling against his visor.

Suddenly Cosmo was spat out of the tube's end, his stomach lurching as he fell through air then landed again with a splash. He sank, tumbling and twisting, into the deep channel of another blood vessel. He kicked his legs and swam to the surface, where he heard two more splashes, then Nuri and Brain-E bobbed up too. "Are you two OK?" he called to them.

Nuri gave a thumbs-up. "We must be way inside the planet now."

Brain-E clambered onto a floating golden fruit for buoyancy, stalk eyes swivelling.

Baboom ... baboom ... baboom, echoed Balaz's heartbeat, louder than before.

"It sounds as if we're getting closer to the heart," Cosmo said. "Come on — let's try to get to dry land." He kicked for the shore, but heard a swish of wings and a shadow passed across him as something flew overhead in the gloom. "What was that?" He shone his torch upwards.

There came a splash, then a creature flew through Cosmo's torch beam. It was large and bird-like with feathered wings, and in its clawed feet it held one of the golden fruits. He saw another creature fly down and pluck a fruit from the blood.

Cosmo's torch beam reflected on dozens of pairs of eyes watching from the walls. He spotted more creatures perched

on ledges. They had almost human faces
and some were munching on the golden
vine fruit. "What are they, Brain-E?"

But before Brain-E could reply, one of

the creatures swooped down and plucked
the brainbot from the river.

"No!" Cosmo cried, seeing his friend
being carried away.

CHAPTER SIX

THE SU-BO

The creature flew to the river bank where it perched, turning over Brain-E in its claws.

"Help! It thinks I'm fruit!" Brain-E cried.

"Don't eat it!" Cosmo called, scrambling up the river bank to help his friend.

But the birdman stared at Cosmo, clearly not understanding him. *He's not wearing a wordsworm*, Cosmo realized.

The creature's wings were wrapped around him like a cape, his face like that

of an old man, pale and wrinkly. *"Ungab dongu?"* he said.

Cosmo's wordsworm took a moment to translate the birdman's words, as if he was speaking a rare language: "Welcome, strangers. What is this?"

"Juma div," Brian-E replied from its databank of languages, which Cosmo heard translated a moment later as, "I'm a robot."

The birdman looked puzzled – he had clearly never seen a robot before, and Brain-E quickly scuttled free of his grasp.

"Brain-E, what language is he speaking?" Cosmo asked.

"I don't recognize it exactly, but it's similar to Varusian."

"Try to ask him if he lives down here."

Brain-E spoke to the birdman, "*Yengon verla voolap tok?*"

The birdman replied, "*Ulong Tsune, koola karla ip.*"

"I am Chief Tsuna of the Su-bo tribe," Cosmo's wordsworm translated after a pause. "We have lived here for ever."

Cosmo glanced around: more of the bird people were flying over to see what was going on. "Brain-E, tell him his planet is under attack and we're here to help."

"And that we need to find Balaz's heart fast," Nuri added.

Brain-E translated, "*Ugot goots gaba. Orunab hera kloss. Erba satz clonti.*"

The chief looked at Cosmo curiously, his wrinkled eyes thoughtful. Then he gestured for him to follow, and flew off through a gap in the vein's rock wall. Cosmo, Nuri and Brain-E followed into a dark side tunnel. As the birdman led the way, Cosmo could hear the beating sound

of Balaz's heart growing louder ahead:
babooom . . . babooom . . . babooom . . .

They entered an enormous cavern full
of wild plants and fruit vines, insects
buzzing among them. A phosphorescent
light glowed from moss on the walls, and
in the cavern's centre stood a massive
heart-shaped rock, pointed at the bottom
and broad at the top. Chief Tsuna led them
over to it. The rock was throbbing; large

rocky veins and arteries led in and out of it.

The chief spoke, translated by Cosmo's wordsworm: "This huge rock contains Balaz's heart."

As Cosmo listened in wonder to the heart's rhythm, he heard another sound getting louder too – an engine!

"Look!" Nuri cried, pointing to the far end of the cavern. Rocks were falling from above as the spinning metal tips of two

drills burst through the cavern's ceiling.
The head of a monstrous machine-like
alien peered in, its eye-lights smouldering
red in a caged metal skull.

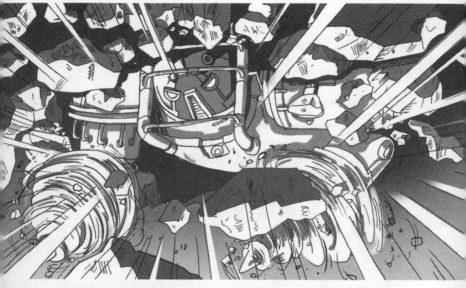

The invader dropped to the ground,
making the cavern quake. He stomped
towards the rock containing Balaz's
heart, his drills spinning.

Cosmo took a deep breath, gathering
his courage. "Stop right there, Minox!" he
called. "I'm Cosmo Santos, G-Watch agent."

The massive alien faced him. "Get

away, boy. I've drilling to do," he growled.

Chief Tsuna clung to Cosmo fearfully. "How can we stop that thing?" he asked.

"Nuri, keep the chief safe," Cosmo said. "It's time for me to mutate and fight!"

He spoke into his helmet's voice sensor, "SCAN!" On his visor's electronic display, aliens flashed in front of his eyes as the Quantum Mutation Suit scrolled through its databank: a mind-bending cyclops . . . a flint-eyed wrath . . . a five-headed spittox . . . *What can beat Minox?* he wondered. He spotted a fierce-looking alien with bony body plates and sharp spiked fists:

ALIEN: GOR
SPECIES: COMBATON
ORIGIN: PLANET ATTAX
HEIGHT: 10.2 METRES
WEIGHT: 2.1 TONNES
FEATURE: SPIKED PUNCH

A spiked punch will split that metal invader open. He spoke the command into the helmet's voice sensor: "MUTATE!"

CHAPTER
SEVEN

GOR THE COMBATON

The power inside Cosmo surged through him, activating the Quantum Mutation Suit. His body tingled, its molecules vibrating as the suit fused with his flesh. He grew huge, with hard bony plates forming across his body. Sharp spikes emerged from his knuckles then along his arms and shoulders. He clenched his spiked fists like awesome weapons, and advanced on Minox. He threw a punch at the alien.

"Aargh!" Minox roared with anger as Gor's fist pierced his metal casing.

Cosmo hit out again, this time tearing open the invader's metal cage. Silver metallicon flesh bubbled from inside, and Minox staggered back in shock, resting his drill arms on the ground to steady himself.

Cosmo struck again, pulling loose a metal pipe from the alien's shoulder with a hiss of steam. Then he punctured the alien's oil tank, and black oil leaked out. "You're finished, Minox!" he said.

"Talk to the drills, G-Watch boy, because I'm not listening!"

Minox's bubbling silver metallicon flesh was solidifying, healing his wounds, soldering them closed again! Ferociously, he thrust a drill at Cosmo.

Cosmo blocked the mighty blow, but its force deadened his arm and it dropped numbly to his side.

With Gor's guard down, Minox quickly jabbed again, striking Cosmo's bony breastplate. Cosmo staggered back, feeling the alien's awesome drill power vibrating against him. He swung a wild punch, trying to defend himself, but the blow missed.

Minox laughed. "It's over, Earthling!" He attacked with both drills, shattering Gor's breastplate and sending him flying backwards against the rock containing Balaz's heart.

Cosmo felt numb; the Quantum Mutation Suit was failing. But Minox was still coming for him.

"RESET," Cosmo gasped, realizing he could not defend himself. He mutated back into an Earthling boy, his back pressed against the throbbing rock of Balaz's heart. He felt it beating faster, as if Balaz could sense the danger too.

Minox's eyes blazed in his caged skull. "Out of my way!" he roared.

"SCAN!" Cosmo said into his helmet's voice sensor. Images of other aliens flashed before his eyes as his Quantum Mutation Suit scrolled through its databank: a pike-toothed lidon . . . an ice-breathing chak . . . a flaming comet moth . . . He saw an alien with a body of vulcanite, one of the hardest minerals in the galaxy.

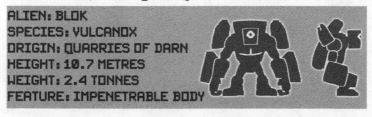

ALIEN: BLOK
SPECIES: VULCANOX
ORIGIN: QUARRIES OF DARN
HEIGHT: 10.7 METRES
WEIGHT: 2.4 TONNES
FEATURE: IMPENETRABLE BODY

Nothing will get past Blok's impenetrable body, Cosmo thought. "MUTATE!"

CHAPTER
EIGHT

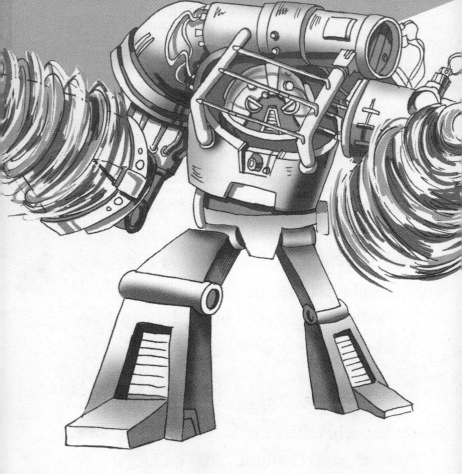

"BLOCK THIS!"

Cosmo's skin tingled as his molecules
mutated into those of Blok. His body
hardened to vulcanite and he grew huge;
his chest and limbs becoming solid blocks.

He positioned his huge bulk in front
of the heart's rock wall and faced the
invader. "There's no way past me, Minox."

"Wanna bet?" the invader roared,
raising his drill arms. He charged, and
Cosmo braced himself for the impact. With

a deafening *CLANG!* Minox's spinning drills struck Blok's vulcanite stomach. Cosmo shuddered but didn't budge.

The drills spun so fast that their tips smoked as they ground against Blok's hard flesh. Faster and faster they whirred, but still Cosmo held his ground. "Is that the best you can do, Minox?"

The drills were glowing red-hot now, sparks flying. They made a whining screech as they tried but failed to penetrate Blok's body.

"What are you made of, freak?" Minox roared angrily. He raised his drills and thrust them against Blok's chest. Again the drills smoked and whirred, but couldn't pierce Blok's vulcanite flesh.

"You're not getting past me," Cosmo said.

Minox tried to charge past him, but Cosmo repositioned himself, stepping in the alien's way. "Give up!" he said, pushing the invader back.

"No way," Minox roared. "Try to block this, you great big blockhead." He began revving his engines, belching thick black smoke from his exhausts. Great clouds of it rose around him.

Cosmo blinked, trying to clear his eyes. He couldn't see in the smoke! He heard Minox's drills whirring, and reached out, trying to pinpoint the sound. "Hey – where are you?" he shouted.

"I'm right here!" Minox taunted. "Shame you can't see where *here* is!"

Cosmo felt the ground shake beneath his feet as though Minox was drilling into it. Suddenly it gave way beneath him; one of his massive legs plunged into a crack in the floor.

"Got you, you fool!" the invader roared.

Cosmo tried to heave himself out but he was too big and heavy – Blok's enormous leg was trapped in the rock!

"Nothing can beat me!" Minox yelled.

As the smoke cleared, Cosmo saw the invader moving towards the rock encasing Balaz's heart, his drills spinning.

"Leave Balaz alone!" Cosmo hollered, but he could do nothing to stop the alien now. Minox pressed his drills to the rock.

"You heard him!" a voice called from above. It was Nuri, flying on the back of the winged Chief Tsuna. She opened fire with her phaser gun, blasting Minox with a round of phaser beams.

"Nice one, Nuri," Cosmo called.

Minox turned angrily, the phaser beams sparking off his metal body. He swung his drill, trying to swat her, but the chief veered away.

"RESET!" Cosmo said, mutating back into a boy. He began trying to shift the loose rocks around him.

Nuri was doing her best to blast the invader, drawing his attention away from the heart. She fired again as the chief swiftly circled Minox.

"*Su-bo doa takka!*" Chief Tsuna yelled.

More Su-bo tribespeople swooped into the cavern, a whole squadron coming to the defence of Balaz's heart. They clawed at the metallicon, trying to tear pipes and cables off his machine-like body.

Brain-E leaped from one of them, landing on the invader's caged skull. Cosmo saw the brainbot crawl down Minox's shoulder, popping bolts and opening panels.

"Way to go, Brain-E!" Cosmo yelled as he pulled his foot free and rushed to help.

The alien roared in rage, hot steam spouting from his pipes, blasting the flying Su-bo.

Nuri fell off Chief Tsuna's back and hit the ground. Cosmo scrambled to her side, shielding her from Minox with his body. "Are you OK, Nuri?"

The invader pointed a spinning drill at them. "Prepare to die, G-Watch wimps!"

But as Minox thrust the drill forward, it spluttered and stopped. The invader looked at his drill arm, confused – there was something wrong with its workings.

"Run, Miss Nuri! Run, Master Cosmo!" a little voice called.

Minox tensed his metal muscles, and suddenly Brain-E popped out from under a panel on the alien's drill arm.

"Get away from me, robot!" Minox bawled, realizing that the brainbot had been blocking the motor to his drill.

Brain-E scuttled over the rocky ground and hid in a crevice as Cosmo helped Nuri across the cavern.

"Thanks, I'm OK now," she said.

Minox's drills started spinning again.
"Enough of your meddling! You cannot
stop me!" He spun round and slammed
both drills into the heart's throbbing rock
wall, trying to break it open.

Baboom . . . baboom . . . baboom . . . the
heart beat, faster and faster.

I've got to stop him, Cosmo thought
desperately. "SCAN!" he said.

Once more, images of aliens scrolled
across his visor. He saw an ogre-like alien
dripping with steaming slime.

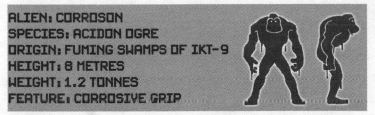

ALIEN: CORROSON
SPECIES: ACIDON OGRE
ORIGIN: FUMING SWAMPS OF IKT-9
HEIGHT: 8 METRES
WEIGHT: 1.2 TONNES
FEATURE: CORROSIVE GRIP

Corroson's corrosive grip might do it,
Cosmo thought. "OK, Minox, prepare to
melt! MUTATE!"

CHAPTER NINE

CORROSON

Cosmo's Quantum Mutation Suit glowed, his body tingling as his molecules mutated into those of Corroson. He grew large and muscular, his skin turning rough and flaky like rust – orange, yellow and red in colour. He flexed his muscles, and steaming acidic slime oozed through pores in his skin, dripping down and hissing as it hit the ground.

He headed towards Minox. The invader's

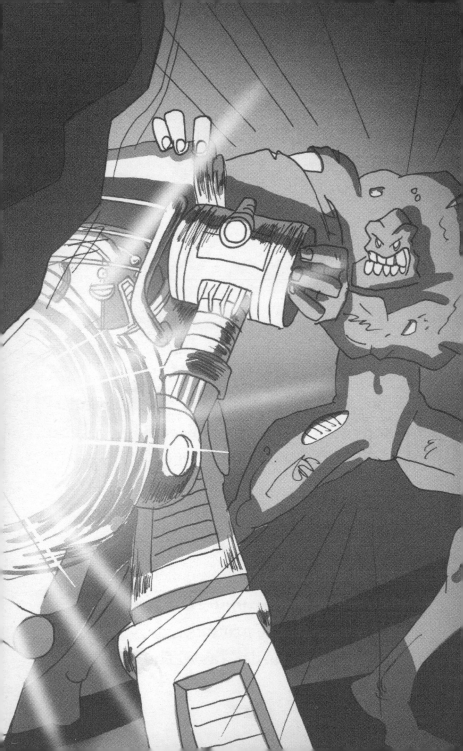

spinning drill was pressed against the rock encasing Balaz's heart, chunks of rubble flying in all directions. Suddenly the protective rock split open, exposing the fleshy black muscle inside.

"Ha ha!" Minox laughed, ready to deal the fatal blow to pierce the heart's flesh.

Cosmo dived at Minox and yanked the invader backwards. He leaped round, putting himself between the invader and the heart. "That's enough, Minox!" he said.

"Oh, but I'm having such a CRACKING time!" the invader roared, and he pushed forward again, trying to drill past Cosmo.

But as Corroson, Cosmo was strong. He grabbed hold of Minox's drill arms, holding them back, stopping the invader from drilling Balaz's heart.

"You can't hold me for ever," Minox sneered, revving his engine harder, sending his drills into overdrive. They spun ever faster, reaching for the cracked rock and the heart inside it.

Cosmo could feel Balaz's heart beating behind him. He tightened his grip on Minox's drill arms, and corrosive acidon ogre slime oozed from his fingers, leaking onto the invader's metal casing.

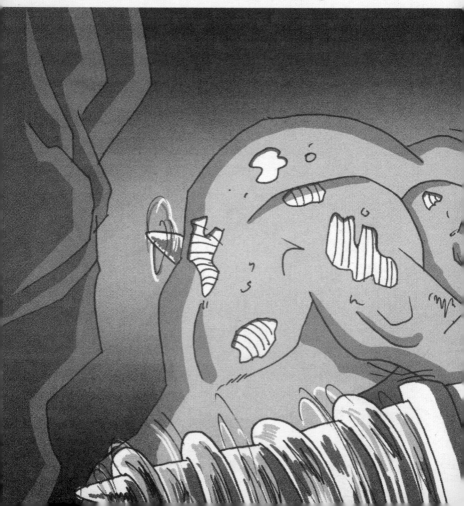

Minox pushed with all his might, his whirring drills just centimetres from the heart now. Cosmo's grip slipped a little.

"I'm too strong for you!" Minox roared.

But still Cosmo held him, Corroson's acid now working its way deeper into the invader's body.

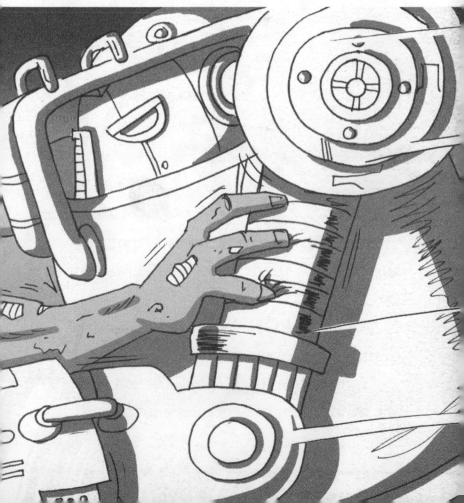

Minox revved harder and his drills rotated faster, but Corroson's acid was now dissolving his metal flesh, burning its way into his arms.

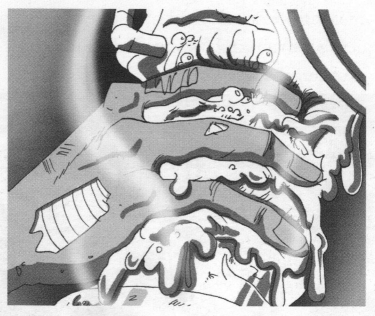

Suddenly one arm melted right through and its drill spun off, crashing to the ground.

"AAAAAARGH! What have you done to me?" Minox roared, his eyes blazing.

"Your time's up, Minox!" Cosmo clung to the other arm, his corrosive grip melting through it, until its drill came away too.

He thumped the metallicon with both fists, forcing him away from the heart. Each punch left a dent in Minox's body, melting his metal casing. "It's over, Minox."

The invader's body began leaking oil, and steam hissed from his damaged pipes. His joints sprang apart as Corroson's acid liquefied his rivets and

bolts. He staggered, malfunctioning, his wiring and circuitry starting to melt.

"RESET!" Cosmo said, mutating back into a healthy Earthling boy. "Minox, it's time for you to leave this planet."

"N-n-noooo waaay-ay-aaay," the invader replied, his voice box disintegrating. With the last of his strength, Minox lunged, trying to headbutt Cosmo with his caged skull, but Cosmo stepped aside, easily avoiding him, and the alien toppled to the ground.

"Say goodbye, Minox!" Cosmo told him. He felt his power welling up inside him and his Quantum Mutation Suit flashed with energy. His arm tingled as the power extended from his gloved hand to form a lightning-like sword – the power sword. "The power of the universe is in me!" Cosmo cried, plunging it into Minox.

He shuddered as his power battled for supremacy with the invader's: his life-

force versus Minox's evil. The alien's melting metal body began to shudder. His eye-lights cracked and burst; then, in a flash of white light, the invader exploded.

Cosmo staggered backwards with the

force of the blast, overcome with exhaustion.

"Cosmo, are you OK?" he heard. It was Nuri, running towards him across the cavern. She held him in her arms.

Cosmo slumped against her. "We did it, Nuri," he gasped. "We saved Balaz."

He looked for Brain-E, and saw winged Su-bo tribespeople flying overhead. The brainbot was hitching a ride and flashing its lights in victory. "Hooray, Master Cosmo!" it called.

Cosmo smiled with relief, seeing that Nuri, Brain-E and the Su-bo people were safe. He turned to the planet's heart. It was still beating soundly, its outer protective rock only superficially damaged.

Chief Tsuna landed beside Cosmo. *"Unga dosin lagan dagai,"* he said.

The wordsworm in Cosmo's ear translated the winged chief's words. "Thank you for saving our planet. May I offer you a lift back to the surface?"

Cosmo smiled as the chief spread his wings. He glanced at Nuri. "Let's get back to the Dragster and radio G1 with the good news."

* * *

In the cockpit of the battleship *Oblivion*, Kaos checked the computer monitors, his five heads pale with shock.

"Minox has failed!" his first head said.

"I don't believe it . . ." his third head muttered. Kaos turned dials and flicked switches. "Maybe there's something wrong with the equipment."

The scanners from Minox's brain and heart were flatlining. Kaos pressed a

button bringing up the final signal from the camera behind the alien's eyes. On the screen was an image of Cosmo holding the power sword.

"That blasted Earthling boy has done it again! The G-Watch brat! He's defeated Minox!"

The four other heads all scowled at the third. "*Your* plan wasn't so 'foolproof' after all," they spat.

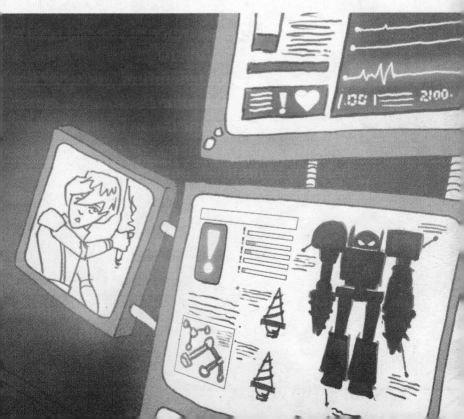

The door from the corridor opened and Wugrat entered, exhausted, wheeling in a steaming cauldron. "Eeek eeek eek," the rat squeaked.

Kaos's first head scowled. "No, Wugrat, now is *not* a good time for the victory feast!" He kicked the cauldron and sent critter stew spilling across the floor.

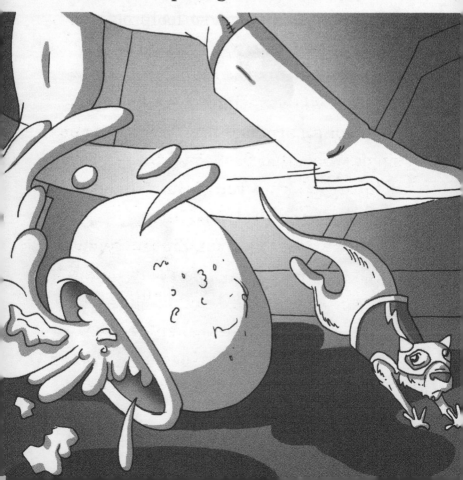

"I believe it's *my* turn now to send in an invader," Kaos's fourth head piped up. "*I* am going to send in Zipzap!"

Kaos grabbed an electronic circuit board, and his heads all looked at each other. The fourth spoke: "With the invasion plan *I've* encoded on this circuit board, *my* invader will bring the galaxy to its knees, and that meddling G-Watch boy will wish he'd never been born!"

Kaos swept into the cargo hold, where two aliens were waiting: one with a huge cannon for an arm and the other riding on a single wheel that flashed with electricity.

"Zipzap, it's your turn," Kaos's fourth head said to the electrified alien.

"Yes, Master," the alien, Zipzap, replied.

"Turn round so I can insert your orders."

Zipzap turned round and Kaos reached up to open a panel in the alien's back, exposing circuitry and silver metallicon flesh inside. He thrust the circuit board

into the hole and, in a sparking flash, Zipzap's soft metallicon flesh absorbed its wires and microchips.

Wugrat scurried in with a navicom transporter disc in its mouth. Kaos snatched it up, turned the navicom's outer ring to set its coordinates, then fastened it to the one-wheeled invader. "Are you ready to ride, Zipzap?" Kaos's fourth head asked.

"Yes, Master," Zipzap replied. He revved his engines, spinning his wheel fast on the spot, making it screech as the roof of the cargo hold opened.

"You'd better not disappoint me, Zipzap," Kaos's fourth head said menacingly.

The invader's eyes flashed cold blue. "I will electrocute all who get in my way, Master," he replied.

The navicom started to flash, and with a *whoosh,* Zipzap shot out into space.

CHAPTER
TEN

TWO MORE TO COME

The three G-Watch friends clung to the back of Chief Tsuna as they soared up through shafts and tunnels to Balaz's surface. Cosmo squinted in the daylight, and saw the Dragster parked by the research ship of Professor Vorp. The professor and his explorobot, R6, were inspecting rocks in Minox's impact crater.

Nuri breathed the fresh air. "It feels good to be back in the open," she said, climbing down from the chief's back. "Goodbye, Chief. It's been great to meet you."

"Goodbye, Chief Tsuna," Brain-E repeated in the chief's language.

The chief smiled and waved and they headed for the Dragster.

"Nuri, Brain-E, would you get the Dragster fired up while I introduce the chief to the professor." Cosmo had noticed Professor Vorp looking over, surprised to see them all.

"How did you get on, Cosmo?" he called.

"Minox has gone, and Balaz is safe again," Cosmo shouted back. "There's someone I'd like you to meet." He led the chief to the crater's edge. "Professor, this is Chief Tsuna. He lives underground with his tribe. If R6 can translate for you, then the chief can tell you all about Balaz."

"I can do that," R6 said.

Professor Vorp bowed his head to the chief. "Pleased to meet you."

"*Oogs chaka*," the chief replied.

Professor Vorp then smiled at Cosmo. "I have some splendid news for you too. Balaz truly is a marvel. Look . . ." He pointed at the ground. Cosmo noticed thin red feeler shoots moving in the crater, meshing together over the rocks like a scab. "Balaz is healing itself," the professor said. "I do believe it'll be as good as new soon – thanks to you, Cosmo."

Cosmo felt proud to have helped in

Balaz's rescue. "All in the line of duty," he replied. "Well, goodbye, Professor Vorp. Goodbye, Chief Tsuna."

The professor held out a pincer to Cosmo. "Goodbye, and thank you for saving this Great Wonder of the galaxy."

The chief folded his wing around Cosmo's shoulder. "Thank you," he said.

Cosmo headed for the Dragster and climbed aboard. On the communications console he saw the face of G1. Agent Nuri

was already telling him the good news.

"Congratulations, Agent Supreme," the silver-eyed chief of G-Watch said, seeing Cosmo taking his seat. "You have shown courage worthy of your rank." G1's face darkened. "But just as we feared, our deep-space scanners have now detected a fourth metallicon invader on its way into the galaxy. Identified as the monorider Zipzap, he is on a direct course for System Opex, where the great Rawbone Rally is taking place. You must go after him."

"The Rawbone Rally!" Cosmo said, surprised. He was a big fan of galactic rally racing. "I'll do my best."

"I know you will, Cosmo," G1 replied. "Over and out!"

The monitor went blank, and Cosmo powered up the Dragster's thrusters, lifting the spaceship off into the sky.

Three aliens down. Two to go, he thought determinedly. "Zipzap, here we come!"

INVADER ALERT!

As dawn broke over System Opex, Galactovision's holographic sports commentator, Rocco Wang, stepped among the line-up of rally vehicles at the start of the 207th Rawbone Rally. He faced a tiny hovering camera, his digital body flickering. "Thanks for tuning in, folks! The suns of Opex are rising and the drivers are ready to go. Welcome to the toughest land race in the galaxy!"

The light from Opex's first sun cast a red glow over the vehicles as they revved their engines: X-trucks, skidrons, armoured carts, roadsters, firebikes, dirt racers; their rugged riders the very best from the galactic sport of extreme rally racing. Galactovision's flying-eye cameras, called galactocams, zipped through the air on tiny wings, beaming images live to the people of the galaxy.

"In pole position is the reigning champ, Axel Crock!" Rocco exclaimed, edging to a chain-wheeler at the front of the grid driven by a bull-horned man. "Hey, Axel, do you think you can win again and beat your rivals, Zimla Cordosa and Ji-Phon?"

Axel Crock coolly revved the chain-wheeler's engine and exhaust smoke billowed around Rocco.

"I'll take that as a *yes*," the commentator smiled, fanning the air with his holographic hands.

Rocco Wang was well known to racing fans: a lifelike hologram in a purple space suit who had commentated on every Rawbone Rally in living memory, his digital body unaffected by the 800 kilometres of hostile planetary conditions that the racers had to contend with.

He glanced up excitedly as the second sun of Opex rose above the horizon, signalling the start of the race. With a roar of engines and a screech of tyres, the rally cars accelerated from the starting grid, dust and exhaust fumes filling the air. Rocco dashed to the sidelines among the emergency support vehicles. "They're off, folks! The 207th Rawbone Rally is underway!"

The rally cars sped towards the Moving Mountains of Antram. As the mountains shifted, gorges opened and closed between them, providing temporary routes through for the fastest drivers. The racers jostled for position, pursued by galactocams.

Rocco Wang shouted above the noise: "The drivers will have to brave moving mountains, ice blizzards, scorching deserts and even active volcanoes. First to the Pillars of Rawbone wins." A wild storm rumbled overhead. "The conditions are *fierce* today, folks!"

Suddenly there came an almighty thunderclap and the sky flashed as something like a lightning bolt landed among the racers, gouging a large crater in the ground. Rally cars swerved to avoid it, crashing into each other and flipping over, tyres and metal flying off.

"Jeepers! What was *that*?" Rocco yelled, hurrying to the scene of the crash. His holographic body flickered with electrostatic interference, then warped as a huge machine-like creature rose from the crater on a single spinning wheel.

"*Whoa!* Who's *that* guy?" Rocco exclaimed.

The machine-like alien sparked with electricity. Bolts of lightning shot from his metal hands blasting passing rally cars. "I am Zipzap," he roared, "and I will FRY you all!"

CHAPTER ONE
SYSTEM OPEX

Cosmo pulled back the throttle of the Dragster 7000 spaceship, blasting through the galaxy's Alpha Quadrant towards System Opex. "Awesome, we're going to the Rawbone Rally!" he said excitedly to his Etrusian co-pilot, Agent Nuri. "I've watched it loads of times on Galactovision."

"Me too," Nuri replied, looking up from the navigation console. "The racers are cool! Zimla Cordosa's my favourite."

From the control desk, the ship's brainbot, Brain-E, bleeped anxiously. "The rally will already be underway," it said. "I do hope the racers are OK."

Cosmo frowned, remembering he was going to the Rawbone Rally not as a sports fan, but as a G-Watch agent on a mission to fight the alien invader, Zipzap. "Brain-E, see if you can tune into Galactovision for the latest rally news. Let's hope nothing bad has happened."

The brainbot began searching the frequencies on the ship's communications console as Cosmo powered the Dragster onwards through the galaxy.

"What's up with the signal, Brain-E?" Cosmo asked, seeing fuzzy video images flickering on the ship's monitor.

"Galactovision's transmission appears to be having some kind of problem," Brain-E replied.

"That's not a good sign," Cosmo said, glancing nervously at Nuri.

"Approaching System Opex now," she said. She tapped the Dragster's spacescreen, activating its star plotter, and words lit up on the glass, labelling the astral objects in view: COMET RAPTOR, NEWTON'S NEBULA, the twin stars ECHELA and ECHELO, and, in the distance, an enormous, irregular-shaped celestial body marked SYSTEM OPEX. The strange mass had been formed centuries earlier when a solar system imploded and its planets collided with one another to create a single huge mass of shifting landscapes and climates. It was the perfect environment for the toughest all-terrain land rally in the galaxy.

Brain-E bleeped from the communications console. "The signal's coming through now, Master Cosmo."

As Cosmo powered the Dragster between the twin stars Echela and Echelo, a video image of Galactovision's holographic sports commentator, Rocco Wang, appeared on the monitor.

"Sorry for the interruption in our transmission from the Rawbone Rally, folks, but some of our equipment has short-circuited," Rocco Wang said. "There's been a pile-up of vehicles at the start of the rally – a racer calling himself Zipzap has caused carnage down here. I've never seen anything like it!"

On the monitor, Cosmo saw destroyed vehicles behind Rocco, then the image wavered as the signal was lost again. "Zipzap's attacked the racers!" he exclaimed, blasting towards Opex's misshapen mass. Cosmo summoned his courage for the fight ahead and his spacesuit began to glow. "What do we know about this invader, Brain-E?" he asked.

The brainbot swivelled its stalk-eyes. "Well, according to G-Watch probes, Zipzap is an electric speed-freak, Master Cosmo, able to generate lightning bolts from his supercharged body."

Yikes! So he could electrocute us! Cosmo thought, alarmed. He gripped the steering column tightly and the Dragster 7000 shot through System Opex's outer atmosphere into swirling winds. Cosmo struggled to keep control as the ship bounced up and down in high turbulence.

"Opex's weather is violent and changeable, Master Cosmo," Brain-E warned, sliding across the control desk as the spaceship juddered.

"The rally's start is southeast of here," Nuri said, checking the navigation console.

Cosmo adjusted course, flying the Dragster through a shower of hail stones; abruptly the hail ceased and blinding sunlight flooded the cockpit. Cosmo squinted, but then the spacescreen darkened as black storm clouds engulfed the Dragster. Conditions were changing rapidly. Visibility was almost zero.

Cosmo glanced at the navigation console and saw the Moving Mountains of Antram, the starting point for the rally, indicated below. "We're nearing the strike site. I'm taking us down," he said. "Look out for Zipzap."

As the Dragster descended through the clouds, Cosmo peered through the spacescreen and saw wreckage below: a huge crater in the ground and vehicles overturned, sparking with electricity. There was no sign of Zipzap, but as the spaceship touched down on the planet's surface Cosmo spotted Rocco Wang interviewing racers who'd crashed out of the rally. He turned off the Dragster's engines, opened the cockpit door and climbed out to talk to the holographic commentator. "Mr Wang, we're from G-Watch," he called. "What exactly happened here?"

Rocco Wang glanced at a small winged camera hovering beside him. "A G-Watch agent at the Rawbone! Things are even more serious than I thought, folks!" he announced. He turned to face Cosmo. "A crazy rider calling himself Zipzap entered the race, that's what happened! He knocked out eight cars!"

"That rider's an alien invader sent by a galactic outlaw called Kaos," Cosmo explained, noticing more galactocams flying overhead, broadcasting his every word to the galaxy.

"You heard it here first, folks," Rocco Wang said, speaking to the galactocams. "The last-minute entrant is an alien invader. Which means one thing for this year's racers: DANGER!"

Cosmo looked across the trail of damaged vehicles to the Moving Mountains of Antram. The narrow gorges between them were moving continually, sending rocks tumbling down their sides. "Nuri, we've got to go after Zipzap before he causes any more harm," he called.

Nuri and Brain-E were checking out a dented DAX all-terrain buggy that had been toppled in the strike. Its ape-like Virilian driver and navigator were being treated by a rally ambulance crew.

"Nice car," Nuri said to the driver. "Can we borrow it?"

"Its ignition's blown," he replied gruffly. "It won't start."

"Allow me, Miss Nuri," Brain-E said, scuttling up onto the rally car's dashboard and inserting a probe arm into its controls. With a roar the DAX's engine started and the Virilian driver stared, open-mouthed with surprise.

"We'll bring it back in one piece," Nuri said to him. She winked at Cosmo. "You drive. I'll navigate."

Cosmo jumped into the driver's seat. With Nuri beside him and Brain-E on the dashboard, he gripped the rally car's steering bar and pressed his foot down hard on the accelerator. "We're coming for you, Zipzap!" he yelled as the DAX sped towards the mountains. "G-Watch is entering the race!"

Find out what happens in
ZIPZAP – THE REBEL RACER . . .